THE HOUSE WITH TWELVE ROOMS

First IgniBooks trade paperback edition
ISBN: 978-0-9913717-2-3
This title has been registered with the Library of
Congress.

PRINTED IN THE UNITED STATES OF AMERICA

The House with Twelve Rooms

stories

Stefani Christova

To Ivan

CONTENTS

ABOUT THIS COLLECTION

"Anna's Hair" originally appeared in *Downstate Story*.

"She Believes me…She believes me not…" originally appeared in *Big Bridge*.

"The Coffin with the Eleven-Year-Old Myself" originally appeared in *Grasslimb*.

"Paraskeva's Ghost" and "Suzie Wants to Know the Truth" originally appeared in *Beörh Quarterly*.

"The House with Twelve Rooms" originally appeared in *Raven Chronicles*.

"Mrs. Ripley's Exit" originally appeared in *CT Review*

MRS. RIPLEY'S EXIT

Mrs. Ripley spent the afternoon in her hammock. It was hot and bright under the cherry tree with bare, wide-spaced branches. The tree had suddenly died this spring, and the only reason they hadn't removed it yet was the lack of any other suitable place to hang the hammock. Mr. Ripley had a number of ideas of what they could do next summer about that, but Mrs. Ripley hadn't liked any of them. She wanted her hammock exactly where it had been for the past five years since they brought it from a vacation in Chile or maybe Nicaragua. Besides, the lack of shade was compensated for with an open view toward the sky and with a prolific morning glory that had climbed high up one of the branches.

The afternoon progressed as it usually did on Sundays. The neighbors took turns cutting the grass, shouting hello to each other when they met in the front yards and banging the lids of the trashcans in the alley when they disposed of the clippings. Eventually, the sound of the last lawnmower died away and there was peace.

Mrs. Ripley waited out the din with her book open on her chest and her reading glasses in the grass under the hammock. She watched the blooms of the morning glory fading as the afternoon slipped by and kept an eye on the air traffic.

It was as busy as ever. Shreds of spider web drifted in all directions. Birds flapped black wings, tearing through the webs. Jets popped up from unexpected places in the sky and dragged white tails behind. A dragonfly visited the trumpet flowers, and soon after, the airplane that took the skydivers up could be heard behind the poplars that grew in the churchyard.

Mrs. Ripley didn't feel like getting up and going to the middle of the yard to see the parachutes coming down. She imagined they would do it the same way they always did. Some of the skydivers would float to the ground, white and peaceful like dandelion seeds. Others would make hectic turns, glide sideways, and even spiral around their parachutes. Sometimes, there was the one who enjoyed most the free fall, and his parachute materialized below the others like an afterthought.

Mr. Ripley appeared on the back porch at about 2:30. "Nice legs," he called out to Mrs. Ripley and went back in the house. She studied her bare legs, one of them out of the hammock, pushing her back and forth. Yes, nice legs, long and shapely, brown from the sun on the other side of the

Tropic. Nice hair, too. Green eyes, pretty shoulders, skinny arms.

She tried to think of a use for all those good-looking parts, but couldn't find any. A helicopter she didn't see coming started making circles above the hospital, preparing to land. It did so, and after a very short delay, took off again. Mrs. Ripley groped around for her glasses. She read two pages from the book before abandoning the effort. The glasses went back in the grass and her hand stayed there, too, Mrs. Ripley not having a reason to lift it back inside the hammock. She did so only after the cat wandered by and started licking the inside of her fingers. Mr. Ripley came to the porch one more time and asked if she wanted some tea. She didn't. Maybe a glass of wine? No, thanks. The chopper was coming back. Was it the same one, whoever inside hadn't made it, or was it another one for somebody else, Mrs. Ripley couldn't know.

When she looked away from the helicopter and back in the general direction of the house, there was a rope ladder coming down to the middle of the lawn, ten feet away from her. It must have unfolded only recently because the last few rungs were still shaking. The ladder was spun out of pale, wetly glistening fibers. It went up for about twenty feet, then it seemed to disappear on the white background of a cloud above the chimney, then it was brought back by the blue of the sky, and went up and up until it could not be seen anymore. It was a well-built ladder that could bear Mrs. Ripley's hundred and twenty pounds with ease.

Mrs. Ripley stopped pushing, grew still. The hammock swung in smaller and smaller arches, and came to a full stop. Keeping the ladder in her field of vision, she glanced over the house, the potted plants on the back porch, and the morning glory above her. The blooms, except for one or two, were purplish and puckered, curling inward as she watched. Her whole garden seemed to be folding into itself, murmuring and shifting and getting ready to sleep. Even the sunflowers along the fence didn't follow the sun anymore. Instead, their heads drooped down and followed the lines of the ants passing underneath.

The trumpet flowers sounded, urging her to make a decision. As she hesitated, fine sawdust came down on her face and got into her eyes. The woodworms were claiming the dead tree.

She blinked the dust away and stood up. Her book slid down and landed open in the grass. Without looking, she put her finger in a random place to see if there was a message for her in the book. There wasn't. Her finger had fallen on the white space marking the end of a chapter.

She walked to the rope ladder and pulled a few times. The rope felt moist and cool in her hands, and gave a fresh, green scent. Mrs. Ripley tasted it on the roof of her mouth with a puzzled expression until it came to her what it was. It was corn silk, young and luscious as if just peeled from the cob. She pulled again, this time harder. The ladder didn't give out, and she started climbing. She made it to the fifth rung and looked through the living-room window. The TV was on.

The chair was still carrying Mr. Ripley's imprint, but he was not to be seen. In the corner was the painting she had started right after Christmas. It looked dull and listless, more so than she remembered.

Mr. Ripley had given her the easel, the paints, and the brushes as a Christmas present. He had gotten the best of everything and had cleared the wall above the couch for the picture Mrs. Ripley was going to paint. He wanted something in bright colors, maybe reds and oranges, since the couch in the living room was black, the chairs were gray, and the curtains were pale green when one was in a good mood, but gray and dusty like a moth's wing the rest of the time.

She had decided on a still life with apples and grapes. She had arranged the fruit in an ornate tin platter left from her grandmother. After Mr. Ripley got in the habit of knocking on it with his fingernails, asking how the painting was going, she replaced it with a plain wooden bowl. Then she ate the apples, one by one. The grapes withered in the bowl as no one in the house liked grapes.

Mrs. Ripley looked down. The ladder under her had disappeared. She wasn't very high, perhaps no more than four feet in the air. She could still drop to the grass and go inside to start dinner. On the second shelf in the fridge, the salmon swam in its final pond of herbs and olive oil. In the shadows next to the stove, the turning fork shone with stainless steel ardor. The jasmine rice made tinkling noise as it seeped through a hole on its canvas bag measuring the passage of time with long, white grains.

Mrs. Ripley remained thoughtful for a moment, then, she shrugged and climbed another few steps.

Now she could see through her son's window on the second floor. Her son was at his computer, playing video games. Only the top of his head was visible above the monitor, tufts of untidy dark hair just like her own. The clicks of the mouse came rapid and urgent, which meant that something was dying in the virtual realms, and with any luck, bringing her son closer to his goals. He needed more armor for his character and was trying to get to the next level before the weekend was over, since he had fallen behind his friend Marcus. He had played until two in the morning; she heard him arguing with his father who had turned his lights off.

Mrs. Ripley clung to the ladder for a while and breathed the air coming from her son's room. It was spicy with the unwashed socks under his bed, fruity with the gummy-bears he liked to eat, and papery with the hundreds of comic books spread around. A soft, rustling noise made her look down, and she saw the ends of the rope unraveling under her feet. She took one last breath and moved up until she reached the level of the roof.

From here, she could see all the way down the street. The kid next door was playing with his dog. Mrs. Marshal was watering her chrysanthemums and her pink flamingoes. Mr. Jones was unloading his fishing gear from his pick-up truck.

One more step, and Mrs. Ripley saw her husband. He was washing the car in the driveway, the music coming from his stereo louder than the neighbors would approve of. A blaring, high-pitched solo started, and her husband dropped the hose to play air guitar. He did so in a very credible manner, swaying back and forth, his eyes half-closed, his face crumpled with the imaginary effort of performing on the biggest stage in the world. The water coming from the hose made a rainbow over the concrete. A wholesome, beautiful, miniscule rainbow.

From that high everything looked miniscule—the people, the houses, the streetlights, Mrs. Ripley's life, but her life looked miniscule from any point of view.

She prepared to start up again, when a painful tug at the nape of her neck distracted her. A string of hair got caught up in her necklace. Her husband had given her this necklace when they were still in college. It was made out of dried seeds, kernels and beans, colored with red lacquer. For the past fifteen year, she had always worn it on the first day of autumn. This year she would have forgotten if not for her husband. He had looked at the calendar this morning and said that it was necklace day again, and soon they could go watch the aspens turning color. Mrs. Ripley freed her hair and tried to unlock the necklace. She couldn't do it with one hand, so she pulled hard on it, and the seeds and the beans and the kernels poured down like red rain. One of the kernels fell on the driveway and rolled next to her husband's foot, but he didn't notice and went to turn the water off.

Wind blew. It hurried between the houses, replacing the smells of evening cooking with the strong, grassy scent of cornfields. Mrs. Ripley sneezed in her sleeve, and up the ladder she went, not stopping anymore and not looking down where everything was getting smaller and smaller until it all disappeared in the pearl-gray twilight.

SHE BELIEVES ME...SHE BELIEVES ME NOT...

Tom Ashley sits next to me, needlessly prolonging the uncomfortable exchange we just had. He asked me out, and I refused. What more needs to happen? I have finished saying no. He should get up and leave. Instead, he grows even older. The liver spots covering his balding forehead crawl further up his scalp where coarse, gray hair hasn't made up its mind to fall out yet. An excess of skin folds on his neck. His ear lobes turn soft and droopy, and reach the collar of his shirt.

"Why?" Tom asks, without looking at me, his eyes on the dancing couples. "Please be honest with me and tell me why."

"You are too old for me."

Tom's earlobes shrink. He loosens his tie and speaks, still not looking at me. "I am your sister's age, Lindsey, twenty-nine. That makes me, what? four, five years older than you? What are you talking about?"

The band starts "Come Away With Me," and I see my grandfather pushing through the crowd in my direction. I feel relief, but then I realize that he is going to invite Millie, not me. Millie giggles, covers her face with both hands, and standing up so quickly that she almost overturns her chair, she rushes into my grandfather's arms. He bends over to tie her shoe, his face getting red and his bones screeching. He tightens the other shoelace just in case, and leads Millie to the dancing podium with reverence as if she were his queen.

It doesn't matter that he is the best dancer on the floor and all she can do is tumble her feet in place, lifting them about four inches above the ground and putting them down with a force that makes the adjoining couples pull aside protecting their new shoes and old corns. Soon, there is a wide circle around Grandfather and Millie. She laughs her mute laughter with wide-open mouth, her lower lip and chin glistening with saliva. He takes small graceful steps around her, making it look almost like a real dance. I am missing the moment, but when I look again, he is already a younger man. Not very young—he doesn't seem fond of his youth. When he is happy, he is fifty.

He gains about two inches in height, his hair barely has any gray, and his mustache is black and thick.

I can see through people's time. I am used to it, and it doesn't bother me much. Of course, no one believes me. No one has ever done as little as to comment on my ability even when I do something that makes it obvious. I could say, "Father, why are you so old tonight?" when I see him lying on the couch after work, his reading glasses askew and the paper unread on his chest, and he would only snort a little louder and mumble, "When I was your age, everyone over thirty looked old to me."

But he is fifty-two, and he looks fifty-two most of the time. Only on the evenings when his boss had passed him over for promotion, or he has lost his imaginary gains on the stock market, or my grandmother failed to recognize him again, he would age another twenty years, and lose all his hair, and the skin on his jaws and neck would sag. I would sit on the side of the couch and try to smooth the deep wrinkles on his forehead, and he would chase me away, not suspecting or not believing that I truly see him as an old man.

Sometimes, when my mother is asleep on the lounge in the backyard, I see her in her early twenties, her face radiant like the face of a sleeping child, short hair sticking to her sweaty forehead, her hand patting her belly and her lips twitching in the direction of a smile.

When I looked through her pictures one winter, not those she keeps in the family albums, but the ones she hides in a box in her closet, I saw a picture of her with the same short hair and a huge belly. She dreams herself pregnant with her first child, my brother, who didn't live through his first year.

Poor Mom. No matter what we do, my father and I, we can never make her as happy as she has been back then.

Seeing people's age according to their moods comes with the freight of involvement, with the aftertaste of unwarranted nostalgia, but it hasn't always been like that.

When I visited my grandparents as a child, I had lots of fun playing with my grandmother. The moment she folded her apron and put it next to the sink, she would turn into a girl my age. I remember the first time it happened. We were in my secret garden—on the side of the house, behind the currants—planting snowdrops and crocuses for the next spring. The earth was soft, and we were digging holes for the bulbs. We were both eight. Grandmother's wedding ring kept slipping off her finger. Her hands were plump, but still they were eight-year-old hands and had nothing to do with the arthritic hands with large knuckles of her late middle age. I offered to take the ring to Grandfather for safekeeping, but she refused, and I worried the whole time that she would lose it and we would have to spend hours looking for it, digging out the bulbs we had just planted.

The ring is mine now. She gave it to me before she went to live in the nursing home. She was afraid she would lose it, she said. She still can turn young when I visit and when she knows who I am, but when I leave, she crumbles into such an old age that I know she has many more years to live, not recognizing her own face in the mirror. I look down at the thin, worn-out band, for a short time only, lest it gives Tom an excuse to rekindle the conversation.

Silvia, the maid of honor, comes in my direction, limping and holding up her mauve dress, which she doesn't need to do for any practical reason. Silvia is blue-eyed and blond. Mauve agrees with her complexion much better than it does with mine, and I suspect she had insisted on the color. I wanted apple green.

She heaves a sigh as she takes Millie's chair next to me. She wouldn't sit there if she knew whose chair that had been—she winces at my cousin, repulsed by the drool and the incomprehensible babble, not realizing how much in common she has with the retarded girl.

They are the only two people I know who always remain at one particular age. Millie—whatever is her actual age, Silvia—always forty. Silvia has looked forty since the time I first met her when she must have been twelve. Her prim dresses and abundance of make-up only support the impression, but she looks middle aged even when she is coming out of the pool wearing a swimsuit and only very little makeup of the waterproof kind.

"I am Silvia," she introduces herself to Tom Ashley. "Bride's best friend. And you are…?"

Tom shakes the offered hand, pronouncing his name as if it were a name he had always hated and was planning to change first thing after the wedding. Silvia forgets she was limping and jumps out of her chair when he asks her to dance. As they reach the dance floor the music stops and they need to wait for the next piece, Silvia keeping her head slightly to the left, which she believes shows the prettier side of her face, Tom biting his lower lip. They look good together, both made middle-aged, by disappointment in Tom's case, and pure crabbiness in Silvia's.

The music doesn't start. All of us have missed the announcement that the band is taking a break and a pair of comedians will entertain us instead. The comedians are trying to pull a Laurel and Hardy spiel, not very successfully. No one listens to them. The couples on the dance floor chat with their neighbors for a while, then slowly disperse in search of refreshments. I see my sister talking to Tom Ashley. It works to her advantage that her smile is pretty even when it is fake—I doubt anyone notices that she is pissed. Our eyes meet, and she makes a gesture for me to follow her, taking a turn to go inside the house, without waiting for me to catch up.

Upstairs, she pulls me into the bedroom designated for her use. She whispers, but her voice is jagged and her breath smells like copper. "You selfish little brat...It's always you, isn't it? You couldn't spare me your bullshit...at least on my wedding day!"

"What are you talking about? What have I done?"

"I asked you to be nice to Tom Ashley, remember? You said you would."

"Sorry, I totally forgot about that. Anyway, what could I have done differently? I thought you meant it in a general way, since he is Jim's partner, not in a—"

"Jim is not his partner yet. Tom was supposed to make it official weeks ago, but he seems to be having second thoughts. Did you forget that, too? We talked about it at the rehearsal dinner."

"Hey, don't worry. Tom should be ever so lucky to have Jim as a partner. Jim is the hottest new lawyer in town, isn't he?"

My sister doesn't answer. She weeps in desperation I don't understand. Her mascara is running along with the tears, leaving inky tracks on her face and down her throat. She looks like a child bride in some eastern melodrama who is marrying an older, unloved man.

"What is this really about, Kellie? It can't be about Tom Ashley. It's about Mom, isn't it? She didn't allow you to reschedule the wedding because of her, and you are worried she may be dying, and it's just too stressful for you." I look around for tissue, and not seeing any, step into the adjacent bathroom for some toilet paper. She takes a handful and wipes her face, seemingly calming down, but when she looks in the mirror and sees her red-blotched face, she starts to sob again.

"Kellie, Mom is not dying! She'll be fine. I know it. Didn't you see her? This morning when we went to the hospital? She looked at least eighty."

"Oh, shut up! I don't want to hear any of this nonsense. Of course she's not dying, no one dies from appendicitis. And it's just me in here, OK? You don't need to flaunt your bogus supernatural powers for me. It won't get you any points."

She dabs her eyes one last time and starts to reapply mascara, rotating the little brush as she glides it through the length of her eyelashes. When she is done, she doesn't turn to face me. She speaks like a doctor making an unpleasant but not life-threatening diagnosis. "You are sick, do you realize that? You are worse than Millie. At least she is friendly and lovable. I would rather have her for a sister."

I've never heard this before. I've heard the complete big sister repertoire of what a useless and insufferable piece of sibling I am, but never that. My hands start to shake. I toss the rest of the toilet paper in her direction. The paper doesn't have enough weight to carry through. It unfolds somewhere between the two of us and spirals to the floor. I pick it up and smash it into a denser ball, but instead of hitting my sister with it, I hit the mirror and leave the room.

Downstairs, somebody opens a door. I back into another bedroom and recognize the room I and the other bridesmaids used to change into our gowns. I find my cut-off jeans and the t-shirt on the chair where I had left them, but my sandals are nowhere in view. They are not under the bed or in the closet. The other bridesmaids' shoes are lined up next to the dressing table. I can't remember where I put mine.

I wonder if I'll be able to walk across town in high heels, and think of the dirty parking lot of the hospital, through which I need to pass. Even if I go barefoot the rest of the way, I'll need to put my shoes on in the parking lot to avoid stepping on old gum and spilled ice cream.

When I take the gown off, my hair comes undone on one side, and I pull the rest of it free. Still in my underwear, I smash the gown into a giant mauve ball and leave it in the middle of the bed. I put my casual clothes on, and, shoes in one hand, I tiptoe out of the room, down the stairs, through the front door, and out of the fake colonial house rented for the event.

The flower arrangements on both sides of the door wilt in the afternoon sun. Partially deflated white balloons float at knee level. A single rose from someone's bouquet lies on the ground, crushed under the feet of more than two hundred guests. My father didn't have that kind of money, so Kellie and her future husband took a loan to pay for the wedding. Four-and-a-half percent for five years.

I turn my back on the house and start down the street. My father's car is parked a little ahead and I try the doors, remembering that I was trying the shoes when we arrived and had left my sandals in the car, along with my backpack. The car is locked, of course.

As I take a few steps, a police car with flashing lights pulls next to me. I don't stop, this could have nothing to do with me, but an officer gets out of the car and calls after me. "May I see your ID?"

"Why would you want to see it?" I ask over my shoulder, barely slowing down.

"There has been an increase in crime, and we are making random checks. Your ID, please."

"I don't have it with me." I turn to face him, smiling, expecting him to smile, but he doesn't. He takes out a clipboard and starts writing something down, gradually turning into the short, chubby, double-chinned bully he had been at ten.

Going back to the wedding party and searching for my father so I can ask for the car keys is unthinkable. I try to think of something else, but my mind is blank. The only thought that passes through is: leave me alone leave me alone leave me alone.

"May I have your name, address, and date of birth?" the ten-year-old officer asks, and I want to slap him, to erase his self-important expression, to see the surprise and unbelief on his stupid face.

I take a deep breath, willing to calm down, aware that the sooner I start cooperating, the sooner I'll get out of here. Instead, I speak to him with hatred he couldn't miss even if he wanted to.

"Do I look like a criminal to you? This is a public street, isn't it? Can't I just walk the streets of my own town without being bothered?"

"Miss, your name—"

"No, you give me your name first. I want to see your ID. I want to know isn't there something better for you to do but harass an innocent citizen." My hands are shaking so hard now that I drop the shoes. Instead of picking them up, I step into them. I realize I am swaying like a drunk but cannot help it. I adjust the straps of the shoes and look the officer in the eye. The three-inch heels take me close to his height, which is back to more than six feet. I point a finger at him.

"How do I know you are a real policeman? You could be a homicidal psychopath. Show me your ID!"

"This isn't enough?" The officer gestures towards the car with its lights still flashing, and then to his badge.

"It's not! You may have stolen them."

"Miss!" His eyes are bulging, and he has two dark red spots on his cheeks. He is the most unsightly and unpleasant man I've ever met. He takes his radio out and waves it in my face. "Do you want to do this the easy way or the hard way?"

"The hard way, you bastard!"

"Did you just call me a bastard?"

"No, I called you an ugly son of a bitch."

Two more police cars appear, lights flashing, one of them pulling up next to me, the other climbing the sidewalk.

Suddenly, my sister is here, pushing the officer away. She is screaming and crying at the same time. I want to tell her she will ruin her makeup again, but she turns to look at me and I see her face, swollen and blotchy. On the day of her wedding, my beautiful sister looks like a crime victim. The scene is a crime scene.

A crowd gathers. Women with flowery dresses and big round eyes. Men with wrinkled suits, one size smaller than they ought to be. I don't know any of these people. The only one I recognize is my father. He talks to one of the cops, waving his arms, pointing to the house, to his car, to my sister, who now sobs quietly in Jim's arms.

I know Jim well. I've seen him at least fifty times while he was courting my sister. With his freckled skin, cowlick, and boyish manners, he looks younger than Kellie. Even now, comforting her, trying to hide his emotions—worry, annoyance—whatever they might be, he looks more like a baby brother than a husband. Kellie eases out of his arms and comes to me.

I am sure she will slap my face. I flinch but don't move. Kellie seems to have read my mind. She stops a good distance away from me, and when she speaks, it's hard to hear. "How old is Jim now?" she asks. I don't get it. I take a step closer.

"Why are you asking that, Kellie?"

"Don't play a dummy. This is an easy question. Do you see Jim as an old man?"

"I wish you would explain," I say, and suddenly I know what she is asking. Have I heard whispers about tests being done? Have I noticed something in the way Jim and Kellie look at each other? Have I...

The policemen are talking to my father in what seems a friendly manner. They will leave any moment now. We will need to go back into the house and pick up with the wedding reception. I don't know what to tell my sister. She waits and her eyes are impossible to meet.

"Sorry, sis…I've been making this up…for the attention, you know…. I see what anyone can see. Jim looks great—"

She turns on her heels and leaves me. Her back is humped, her shoulder blades stick out in sharp angles, and under her veil, white hair sprouts in thin wisps. A twenty-nine-year-old Jim rushes after her and takes her hand.

THE COFFIN WITH THE ELEVEN-YEAR-OLD MYSELF

The coffin with the eleven-year-old myself is in the garage. My mom's car is parked next to it, and I am always afraid that when my mom backs out of the garage, she will tip the coffin over. The roots of the cottonwood tree that grows next to the garage had lifted the concrete of the garage floor and created an uneven surface that makes the table with the coffin shaky and the vibrations of my mom's car dangerous. I hear my mom starting her car and keep an eye on the way her maneuvering goes. Everything is fine this time. The coffin shakes just a little, and the glass lid rattles, but not much. Mom leaves in her old station-wagon, not waving good-bye, and I linger around the yard, dread in my heart.

I see the next-door neighbor going in the garage and helping himself to some of the gardening tools in the corner. Can't imagine what he needs them for. The gardening season is over. It is late autumn and the garage is full of dry leaves. They rustle under the neighbor's feet as he rummages around not looking at me in the coffin or me on the back porch. Now he drops something on the floor and leaves it there. When my mom comes back, she will need to get out of the car and pick it up, whatever it is, so she can park. I go in the garage after he is gone and kick away the small garden hoe the bastard had dropped. I don't look in the coffin, either. I know what is in there. A 5' 3", 87-pound girl with flaky, brown skin and long strings of dry hair. Her eyes are closed, and her arms are wrapped around her. She looks like she is hugging herself. The color of her clothes has faded, and there is a good amount of dust all over since the lid is not airtight. "She looks so sad," people say, but the truth is that she doesn't. She has no reason for sadness. She is dead.

I sit on the porch and wait for the time to pass. It does so, gradually taking the day away. The air is speckled with dark, and the backyard, the trees, the neighbors' houses, the sky, and the coffin in the garage look like a scene from an old movie. Or a dream. But I know it's not a dream. If it were, I could've done something to wake out of it, or it would have ended eventually, or I could've changed it a long time ago. Sometimes I can change my dreams. I can do alternative endings when I don't like the ones provided by my subconscious. Last night, I dreamt I was in a room with many doors. I opened one of them and it led to another, smaller room. In the smaller room, there was one door only, and when I opened it, it led to another smaller room. The rooms kept getting smaller and smaller until I was in a tunnel and couldn't turn around and the air started getting scarce. I was about to suffocate when I restarted the dream from the point of the first room and opened another door. It led out to the garden, and my cat was there, playing with his catnip toys. My eleven-year-old self was there, too, reading a book in the raspberry bushes that used to grow in the place of the garage. The garage wasn't built yet back then, and July had the place, making everything glow. Dahlias with giant heads swirled their psychedelic colors. Bees collided in mid-flight, dizzy from the fragrance of the roses. One garnet and one ruby foxglove sang choriambic secrets to each other. Ripe mulberries dropped on the tin roof of the shed, one by one, a sugary drumbeat. Even the young apple tree with sour fruit that didn't earn it a place in the garden for the next year vibrated like a bride, full of good expectations. My eleven-year-old self looked up from her book and smiled when she noticed me. She lifted the book so I could see the title. It was "The

Three Musketeers." "Can I come in? Please let me come in," I whispered to her, the urgency in my voice hot like the sun. "Sorry, not yet. Maybe someday but not today." My eleven-year-old self reached above her head and picked a small green apple. She tossed it in my direction, but I didn't catch it. The scene started closing. The apple tree shook its leaves and threw in the air round, glittery reflections like fishing spinners. The cat rolled in the dust, lifting miniature tornadoes. My eleven-year-old self smeared raspberries on her lips to color them red. One last breath of hot air on my face, and I was alone in the room with many doors.

I close my eyes and I see the room just as I saw it then. My summer garden with the eleven-year-old myself and my cat is behind one of these doors. One other door leads to the tunnel. I don't know where the rest of the doors would take me, and I am not curious. There is only one door I am interested in. I will go there again if I can. I won't have trouble finding the room with the many doors; I can go there any time I want. The trouble will be finding the right door. I should've left it ajar or marked it with chalk when I left my dream, but I didn't think of it. I was thinking of what to say to the girl with the book. What to tell her that would make a difference. Be careful or you'll end up in a coffin in the garage? That didn't seem quite right, and, besides, it would not change a thing.

I check the shirts on the clothesline to see if they

are dry, and think about choices. (My red, long-sleeved shirt flaps in my hands like a bird about to fly away. I don't let it go, it's my favorite.) Most people believe they could change their lives if they were given a second chance. They would open the right door this time and find themselves in the garden where the things they love reside. They would never end up in the tunnel. If it were possible, why don't they do it now? Are all the doors closed by the age of eleven? Oh, their circumstances are preventing them. They have children to feed, wives to take on vacations, mortgages to pay. There is no time now. Did they forget that there was even less time back then? That they had chores to do, and homework to start or to finish, and football to kick, and dreams to dream? Is the excuse that their parents were not insistent enough and never took them to auditions?

My mom's car is just pulling into the driveway. Behind the dirty windows is my mom's angry face. My mom always looks angry in my proximity. She gets out of the car and her expression softens for a moment when she glances over the coffin with the eleven-year-old myself. Then she walks toward me, and her face is angry again.

I don't trust her. In the blackness of the nights tinted with insomnia, I picture her going to the garage with a big sledgehammer. Smash! The lid of the coffin with the eleven years-old myself crushes in an explosion loud enough to wake up the whole town. People turn in their beds and murmur to their spouses, "She's finally done it." "Yeah, it was about time." The splinters from the glass lid are still suspended in the air when my mom delivers the second blow. Brittle bone and dry skin fly out of the coffin to take the vacant spaces between the glass splinters. I weep. Then I try to think of something else, but what else is there to think about?

I know my mom blames it on me. She thinks the skinny, dark-haired girl with dreamy eyes that lies in the coffin is my fault. "You said you will travel the seas on a reed boat just like Thor Heyerdahl when you grow up," my mom calls out after me when I go to my waitressing job at night. "You were going to sing, 'I've just arrived in my fantastic boat!' when you came home for Christmas. And you promised two sun-tanned, bright-eyed children to visit me and tell me stories from the seas. Remember?" I don't answer. What can I say? Is it that my mom had dreamed of being a lab technician, living with a husband who never talks to her and a daughter who waits tables? All those store clerks, bar tenders, administrative assistants, the lady who sells sun-flower seeds in front of the stadium, the fellow who comes to fix the toilet when it leaks, or the woman who works in a nursing home for dying people, did they dream of becoming what they are now? Did the boy next door who plays piano in the bar in the vacuum of no one's attention dream of that when he was dreaming of music? Or what about my best friend from the time we were both eleven? We used to walk hand-in-hand, talking and laughing and feeling absolutely confident that the great things allotted for us were just around the corner. Now she is a tax accountant and she seems content with her life, her husband, and her new curtains on the windows of her new house. But she cannot lie to me. I was there. I was a witness. We used to dream our dreams together, and this wasn't what she was dreaming of. Why there is no coffin in her garage? Or in the basement of her new house? Maybe there is a coffin, but she hides it somewhere where no one can see it.

I need to talk to my mom about that. Is it really my fault that my dreams were so potent that they turned me into a murderer when I couldn't make them come true, or is it just the lack of space? If we had an attic or an extra room where we could put the coffin with the eleven-year-old myself, maybe we would've forgotten about it by now, the darkness would have stopped blemishing the air, I could have hung new curtains on my windows, and she could have put the picture back on the wall. The picture of the skinny girl with raspberry lips, hugging her cat and smiling, unaware of the killer inside her.

RICHARD AND JULIA

At the breakfast table, shortly after Richard had hidden behind his newspaper but before he was too immersed in the sports section, Julia made her announcement.

"I've decided to go mad," she said.

Richard didn't put his newspaper down immediately. First, he let out a sigh, the tiniest sigh, that fusty air kept at the bottom of his lungs for the last two months. He hoped she wouldn't catch it, but he was wrong.

"You sound relieved," she said. "You thought I was having an affair."

Richard finally put the paper down, smoothing the creases and folding the pages with care, as if it were origami. "Yes," he said. "That's exactly what I thought."

"Are you pleased that I am going crazy instead? Or disappointed?"

"Not sure," Richard admitted. "What will your madness consist of?"

Julia didn't know yet. She said that she had run a few possible models through her head, but without the real experience, she couldn't tell what would suit her best. She only knew she wanted to be a different person. Somebody younger, happier, with a still undamaged capacity for dreaming. "I don't seem to get hold of this middle-age thing," Julia complained with unwarranted bitterness as if she were the only one dealing with middle age. As if Richard had easy time watching his hair disappear and worrying about his erections, which, thank God, were fine for now. He listened wearily, Julia's words cutting through sometimes, sometimes not. Only fragments caught his attention. "Being delusional is the closest thing to reality—" Then, "I'll still live here, I'll pretend you are…hmm…I don't know…somebody else, too, I guess." And, "Do you mind if I move out of our bedroom?" And, "I could wear floral-print dresses."

Richard used to hate her bright, red-roses-on-yellow-background dresses, which she wore when they first started dating. He had thought the colors didn't become her and felt a little embarrassed for her.

"Why would you move out of the bedroom?" he

asked.

"You snore, for one thing, and you always complain about my reading light. I will take the spare bedroom downstairs. That way the loud music won't bother you."

"What loud music?"

"You haven't been paying attention! I said, I may choose to go Goth, and if I do that, I'll listen to loud death-metal."

"It won't go with floral-print dresses."

"Unfortunately, it won't," Julia agreed. "And black looks terrible on me. I love the music, though. What do you think I should do?"

Richard looked out the window, at their backyard, where the first finches were pulling worms out of the lawn. That time of the year again. Soon the poor buggers will start hitting the windowpanes, seeking death into the illusive reflection of blue skies and budding trees.

"Isn't it a little too early for you to go mad?" Richard said, turning his attention to the problem at hand. "You've always said you would become an eccentric old lady, but you are far from old age, dear."

"Who is talking eccentric here? I am plenty eccentric as it is, thank you very much. I mean mad, out-of this-world mad. I just need to decide on personality. A rebellious teenager, a sweet debutante, a—"

"It wouldn't make much difference one way or another," Richard said, referring not to the proposed types of madness, but to her being sane or not. "Just don't move out of the bedroom. You can read as late as you wish, I won't say a word." He looked at the grandfather clock on the opposite wall, and was relieved to see that it was time for him to leave for the office.

"We'll talk more about it tonight," Julia said, brandishing her butter knife with enthusiasm that made him feel spent. At eight in the morning, and there were two difficult clients to be taken care of before the end of the day.

That night, Richard found his wife decorating the downstairs bedroom with posters. She had lined the closet's door top to bottom and was pinning more onto the back of the bedroom door. The posters were black-and-white except the fake bloodspots, and depicted long-haired young men with guitars. Some were performing on stage, others posed in churches and cemeteries, or in fantastical decors of dark towers illuminated by full moons and other such nonsense. On the floor was a can of purple paint, which Julia, as it seemed, was planning to use on the walls. The beautiful sage-green walls that they had painted together last summer. Oh God, Richard thought, oh God.

Just then, he heard somebody flashing the toilet, and Josh, or was it Mick, the neighbors' kid, came out still fiddling with his fly.

"Hi there, Mr. Swanson," the kid said. "I am going to steal Julia for the night if you don't mind. Julia, we need to leave on time or we will miss the opening band. Seven o'clock, sharp."

"Where are you going?" Richard asked. "What about supper?"

"No worries," Josh, or Mick, said. "We can eat there. They have chips and stuff. Bye, Mr. Swanson. Bye, Julia, see you in a bit."

Julia waved at the kid, and hung heavily on Richard's neck. "I am so excited," she said. "So, so excited! I am going to my first rock show in ages, and guess who I am going to see?"

Richard's briefcase thudded to the floor. He hadn't realized he was still holding it. He took out a handkerchief—maybe the last handkerchief his wife would iron for him—and wiped his forehead.

"Julia, this is ridiculous. I see you are bored. But going to a concert with the pimply neighbors' kid? Really? This is just too much."

"Would you rather have me go by myself? The crowd at these kinds of events could be unpleasant."

"I don't want you to go alone. I don't want you to go, period. I'd rather see you wear your floral-print dresses."

"You hate my floral-print dresses, Richard. You always have. Now, I need to run. There is some of the last night lasagna in the fridge, or you could order pizza."

When Julia emerged from their bedroom twenty minutes later, Richard was still standing in the middle of the downstairs bedroom, looking at the posters. Had he turned around in time, he would have seen Julia's black lipstick, already smeared a little, and her heavy make-up, caking on her cheeks, emphasizing the fine lines around her eyes. But all he saw was her back in black velvet jacket, the one she kept from her college years, and her short leather skirt from the same era, the color having faded from black to ash-gray. She hadn't had time to shop for clothes, he thought with a perverse satisfaction. The fishnet tights might have been the only new item she had on her.

"Black is not your color," Richard called after her, jeering, but not failing to notice his wife's slender back and long legs. In the falling darkness, his wife looked younger, as if she had transformed herself merely by the power of her will, and had left him behind to deal with old age on his own.

The next morning, Richard woke up with a headache. His nose felt stuffed, too, and for almost half-an-hour he managed to maintain the hope that he was getting sick. When it became clear this wasn't the case, he got into the shower. There was only a sliver of soap left. He used Julia's expensive shampoo to wash, some on his head, and handfuls on his chest, where the hair seemed to have grown thicker and longer and grayer overnight. In front of the mirror, shaving, he felt an impulse to shave his chest hair as well. "Julia is the one going mad," he said to his reflection, "not you... not I," he corrected himself and went to meet the day and his mad wife.

She was still sleeping, her mouth slightly open, her black mascara smeared, her eyelids puffy. She looked better than she had in years. The puffiness had erased the lines around her eyes, and the open mouth gave her a girly, almost childish look. Madness becomes her, thought Richard, not unkindly.

Julia had come home at three in the morning. Richard heard her stumbling on her way upstairs. She came into their bedroom with the clumsiness of a drunk, and fell onto her side of the bed like a log. Richard didn't know if she had reconsidered her idea to abandon him in their king-size bed, or if she simply was too tired and the habit had taken over. Whichever it was, Richard was glad.

He bent over his sleeping wife. To place a kiss on her face? To caress her cheek with the back of his fingers? A whiff of stale beer made him cringe. He hurried to the window. Julia's Lexus was in the driveway, the left wheels partially in the lawn. Richard could see the pillow Julia used to support her back while driving on the passenger side. The driver's seat was pulled as far back as it would go.

She had allowed the neighbors' kid to drive her car, the same car she refused their daughter when she was on a visit, on the pretext that Bonnie has forgotten how to drive on snow. At least, Julia had the sense not to drive intoxicated. But had the neighbors' kid been sober? Richard could not remember at all what the kid's name was. The dirty, little, screwed-up son of a bitch, he thought, imagining the kid's greasy hands around the fine leather of the steering wheel. Richard slapped his fist onto the open palm of his other hand and thundered down the stairs to move the car.

Three hours later, Julia had cleared her things out of their bedroom. Almost all her clothes and shoes were in black plastic bags, ready to be donated, and the few items that she wanted to keep were tossed in a pile on the bed downstairs.

"What about our children?" Richard asked.

"What about them?" Julia said. "Bonnie comes to see us once a year, for Christmas, and the only reason Mary drags Johnathan here every three weeks is because she wants to spend all holidays with her family. The fucking bitch!"

"I thought you loved Mary."

"I thought you loved me, Richard, once upon a

time. Remember how you used to kiss me when you came home from work? You haven't kissed me for years—"

"This is not true. I kissed you just last Saturday, when we had…made love!"

"It wasn't making love. It was a fifteen minutes of friction that led to relief. Your relief, and mine, too, but nothing more."

"God, Julia, you hate me, don't you?" Richard said, stricken. He felt the blood draining from his face, and acid from his stomach rising up his throat. He wanted to turn his back to Julia, and leave this house, and never come back.

He did turn his back but stayed. After a moment, he felt Julia coming closer. She pressed her face against his should blades, and clasped her hands around him. Maybe she didn't hate him. But did she love him? Did he love her? The question mark of love drooped from the white-washed ceiling, almost visible, crooked and dirty of color. I don't have that kind of imagination, Richard assured himself and dismissed the question mark with the power of his incredulity.

"I don't hate you, Richard," Julia said into the folds of his shirt. "I just want you to remember what making love used to mean. It meant the cold linoleum floor in the kitchen of our first house where we made love in the morning after the housewarming party. It meant the orange blanket we took to the beach on the night of our first anniversary. Do not mistake what we do now for that."

"Is this why you want to go mad? The sex is not good enough?"

"No, that is not it. Anyway, it doesn't matter; I am not going to have sex with you anymore."

"Why not?"

"The age difference, you know. I am eighteen now. It won't be natural."

Richard broke the grip of her arms and walked out of the room and out of the house. Passing by the picture window, he caught a sight of Julia. She appeared so small and so lost, that he would have felt pity for her if he didn't feel so lost and so small himself.

Richard spent two hours in the park across the street. Four hours in the pub on the other side of Main. Another forty minutes in the park. His feet hurt. He had realized he was wearing his house slippers when he made his first trip to the pub's restroom. He had noticed the way other patrons assessed him, the men with scorn, the two or three lewd women at the bar, with pity, and he knew they all saw on him the mark of a rejected lover. Strangely, at the urinal when he saw the real reason for their scrutiny—his slightly worn, red-and-grey checkered slippers, he felt more embarrassed. There was nothing to be done about it at that point but have more beer. Now, crossing the park, he was surprised by how uncomfortable his slippers were, how unfit for walking.

The house was dark. Richard didn't have his keys and he walked around to enter through the kitchen door. He changed his mind when he saw the light coming from the guest bedroom window, which was wide open, and the curtains were open, too. He kicked his slippers off and walked on the grass moist with night dew. When he reached Julia's window, he stepped in the gravel at the base of the building, favoring his left heel with the blister on it.

Strong smell of paint hit him before he had the chance to peer inside the room. Two of the walls were dark purple, the other two still sage green. Julia was in bed, propped high on pillows, with a book in her lap. Her reading glasses were low on her nose. Faking madness didn't seem to help presbyopia. Richard smiled. He didn't know what he was going to do next. Had she lifted her eyes at that moment, he wouldn't know what to do or what to say, but when she finally did look up and saw him, he didn't wait for the arch of her eyebrows to reach their highest point or her mouth to form the words of her inquiry. He was already climbing through the window, scraping his knee on the latch, coming heavily to the floor, and limping across the room to his wife's bed.

Kneeling next to the bed, he took Julia's hands and kissed them, first the right one, then the left where her wedding ring had left an indentation in the skin of her finger. Julia abandoned her left hand to his kisses and stifled a yawn with her right, then removed her reading glasses.

She said, "Will you help me paint the rest of the room tomorrow?"

SUZIE WANTS TO KNOW THE TRUTH

Soap bubbles foam around Suzie's hands as she washes the cup, the small plate and the big plate from her dinner last night. Some of the bubbles take off and drift around her in the sun-warmed air, reflecting the world outside and multiplying the kitchen cabinets, the chairs, the table with the orange globe above it, and the phone on the wall. The phone on the wall. Suzie's heart skips. They should call her today, tomorrow at the latest.

The phone makes a short, whirring sound as if it is about to ring, and trying not to make noise with the dishes, Suzie waits to see if it will. When it doesn't, she unplugs the sink and reaches for the towel on the stove door. The towel takes the bubbles away from her hands, and color and sparkle turn into wet spots on the worn-out material.

Suzie smiles an inward smile. What amuses her, even in the midst of self-pity and dread, is the irony of it. Is her wish for escape going to be granted finally, ten years later, when completely forgotten, the bitter taste left in her mouth from the sleeping pills gone, and when all she was looking forward to is the summer vacation and her painting class.

Suzie wants to be brave. She has been brave for three days already. Can she do it for a bit longer? For as long as it takes? She doubts it. The waiting is becoming impossible to bear, the wading through the fog of her days harder and harder. She may need to talk to her sister. She starts in the direction of the phone, but it looks so bloated with bad news that she cannot make herself touch it. She decides to walk. Her sister lives only a few blocks away.

Suzie goes to the entry closet and rummages through her shoes. The shelf has given way, and all the shoes are piled on the bottom. She untangles one of her favorite sandals and looks in the pile for its pair, in the meantime stepping into the shoe she has just taken out. Her foot slips out to the side, and Suzie almost loses her balance. She picks the shoe up and looks at it. The upper part of the sandal, woven from straw-like material, has been cut through with what seems like a sharp knife. The cut has been made on the outer side, close to the sole. Suzie turns the sandal in her hands, wondering how this could have happened, then she drops it aside and pulls out a pair of rubber flip-flops, bright blue and easy to find in the pile. Each of them has its straps cut off the same way. She searches the pile and looks at shoe after shoe that is mutilated, damaged, impossible to wear.

"Father!" she cries, and her father opens the living room door as if he has been waiting for her call, the paper in one of his hands, his eyes big and moist behind his reading glasses. "Has anyone been here? Eileen maybe? With the kids?"

He takes his glasses off to take a better look at her as she sits on the floor surrounded by her useless shoes, her face distraught to a degree he doesn't seem to understand but doesn't question. "I have nothing to wear. What am I going to do?" Suzie whines, and she knows she is whining but cannot help it.

Her father goes back to the living room and closes the door without saying a word. He comes back in a minute holding a hundred-dollar bill, which he gives to her. Not waiting for her thanks, he is gone again to the safety of his armchair.

Pressure builds up behind Suzie's eyelids. She rubs her temples until it hurts. "How about a bit of self-control?" she asks herself. "How about you leave Eileen out of this?" After a few minutes, she feels stronger and leaves the house.

She drives, still barefooted, to the mall and buys a pair of slip-ons. The shoes are a pearl-rose color that will go well with the new dress she is going to wear tonight for the end of the school year dance, but not so well with the summer dress she has on. Done shopping, she drives to campus—she has things to do there and she wants to have lunch in the cafeteria. She likes the cream pies they have and the spicy pockets with feta cheese.

It is already half-past one, but there is a long queue, students, professors, even parents lined up for a last meal before the summer takes them away to their small towns, suburbia, second homes, Paris, the mountains, wherever. Suzie takes a tray and waits her turn. No one comes after her, she is the last one in the queue. The food they have today is better than usual, she can see that when she looks at the other people's trays. Arugula sandwiches, stuffed peppers, crème brulée. When her turn comes, only some of the stuffed peppers are left, and there are no more clean plates at the line. The three women behind the counter turn their backs on her and start cleaning and tidying the kitchen. She waits for them to notice her, but they don't. "Hello, hi there…no more clean plates." "What? Ah, we just loaded the dishwashers, there isn't a single plate left. Sorry." "What about the crème brulée?"

"What about it? It's gone." "But I see some over there." Suzie points at the inside shelves where the crème brulée crinkles its sugary, golden-yellow crust in ovenproof, individual bowls. One of the women comes to the window and closes it in front of her face, without further explanation. Suzie lifts her hand halfway to the window, and stays like that, giddy with confusion, not knocking, her hand in the air, a little tic pulling the corner of her upper lip.

The tower clock downtown chimes two times. The sound is clear and sharp like a thorn, and it startles Suzie into motion. She wanders out still holding the tray until she reaches the first bench and leaves it there.

The campus is like a ghost town. No people, no moving cars, only a few parked in the vast, empty parking lots. Abandoned bicycles line the buildings' entries or are chained to lampposts and trees. It is like that every summer. The students depart in haste and leave their bicycles behind. On the first day of school, the unclaimed ones will be offered in an auction. Suzie glances wistfully at a bright red, foldable bicycle, and goes through her to-do list where two items wait to be crossed out. She returns the key for the biology lab in the administration office, leaves a memo for her adviser on the door of his office, and reads the messages on the board. It's still two-thirty. She goes to the library, where she picks a Spanish magazine to read, checking in the dictionary every word she is not familiar with. She does that until it's time to go home and get ready for tonight.

Suzie barely knows the boy who is taking her to the dance. He has beautiful hands, long and narrow, with delicate fingers like the hands of a piano player. She will ask him if he plays an instrument if she goes out with him a second time. He shows up at her house with a bottle of inexpensive champagne he says she doesn't need to open now—it's a present for her. She insists, however, and they drink it from glasses that had been too long in the cupboard and give the champagne a faint dusty flavor. He drinks very little, he will be driving, so she finishes her glass, then his, and pours the rest in her water bottle to take along. The plastic bottle expands from the carbonation, and by the time they reach the campus, it is inflated like a balloon. The champagne fizzes and spills out when Suzie opens it, and she drinks quickly, laughing and shaking the excess from her chin and her dress.

Inside, she dances with the boy, with other boys, with two of her professors, and with her friend Amy who has had a crush on her since their freshman year. The boy wants to take her home around eleven, but she refuses, she wants to dance until midnight. He says he is glad she is having such a good time. When he drops her off, he doesn't want to come in, he will call her tomorrow. Not tomorrow, she says, tomorrow is not good, the end of the week should be better.

Suzie wakes up on a soft, feathery cloud, surrounded by apple blossoms and blazing blue sky. The peaceful feeling she brought out of her sleep is still with her, a drowsy happiness that could only be experienced at the brim of awakening. She accepts what she sees without questioning it. The apple blossoms seem frozen in space, not a petal moves or trembles, and their stillness gives the impression of a deeper but forged third dimension like in a holograph. There is a cluster of blossoms no more than six inches away from Suzie's eyes, and she examines them closely. The ones that are fully open are pure white, the buds have a tint of pink on the edges. She wants to smell them even though the fragrance is all around her, she has felt it seeping into her dreams all night. She reaches to bring the twig closer and the shift of weight upsets her cloud. Fully awake now, she moves back to firmer ground.

She is on the apple tree that grows behind their townhouse. Someone had built a platform between the branches for the kids to play on. Last night, she brought her down comforter here and fell asleep watching the stars. Her dress is probably all wrinkled now. Suzie wishes she were still sleeping among the flowering branches, breathing the sweet smell and believing she was in heaven. She closes her eyes and tries to make herself comfortable again, but moves the wrong way and almost rolls off the platform. A wonder she has made it through the night without falling down.

At least her shoes must be safe here. No one could have climbed the tree without waking her. She sits up carefully and searches the folds of the comforter for her shoes. Her heart sinks as she pulls them out one by one. They have been cut the same way as her other shoes. Sharp, clean cuts close to the soles. She falls back into her makeshift bed, hugs the shoes close to her chest, and turns onto her side, curling around them. Now the view through the branches is no longer the bright blue sky, but the thinly grassed open space behind their building.

The trees on the other side look peculiar. They have never been that close or that dense or that old and gnarled. Now they are dark and looming, with shaggy curtains of moss draping their limbs. The artificial pond in front of them has turned into a bog. The bog, in the shadows of the trees, is so overgrown that it takes Suzie a moment to notice the two old women sitting in the murky water. For some reason they have taken their clothes off. The skin on their forearms is loose and their empty breasts hang to their waists. Their features are strange. One of them is bold and her head reminds Suzie of a straw mushroom with its shape and color, and with the gray peelings on the sides. The other one has the pasty skin of someone dredged out of the deep. The first woman is seated deeper in the water, and the second one is behind her standing or sitting on higher ground so they seem stacked behind each other like cards from some obscure tarot deck.

Suzie moves aside the branches and looks at the women. She hopes they will go away but they don't. They look at her, unblinking and expressionless.

"What is happening to me?" Suzie cries so they can hear her in the distance. "Who is depriving me of shoes to wear, of food to eat? Tell me."

The women gain an air of satisfaction about them as if they got something long waited for. "She wants to know the truth. She wants to know the truth," they chant, their voices old and cracking and full of mockery. The one behind pulls something from the water and starts smacking it against the closest tree in time with the chanting. Suzie can see what has been brought out of the water with clarity and in the finest of details. It is a skinless fish. The blood vessels on its body are bright red against the gray of its flesh. The mouth with sharp, pointed teeth is opening and closing. A big, frenzied eye makes rounds in its socket. The bark of the tree is deeply cut and ragged, and the fish makes a loud slapping sound when it is brought against it.

Suzie gags and starts to cry. Not letting go of her pretty, ruined shoes, she slides down the trunk of the apple tree. Just in time she notices Mrs. Pelham, the lady that takes care of the grounds, who is sweeping the pavement and the stairs on the side of the building.

"Good morning, Suzie," Mrs. Pelham calls out. "Did you sleep in the tree house? Nice dress you have. Put your shoes on, you'll catch a cold like that."

"Yes, Mrs. Pelham. I will. Good morning to you, too."

Finally, Suzie is around the corner. Loud sobs shake her whole body. She needs to talk to her sister. She will do it right now. She runs past the first and the second entryways, then past the third one where she lives with her father, and where the phone will ring any moment now. The townhouses with their columned porches and flowerpots with geraniums and pansies waver in front of her eyes as if the whole street has gone underwater and she is watching it from a submarine window.

Suzie cannot stop crying. The air is becoming salty and sparse. Soon there won't be enough to breathe.

ANNA'S HAIR

Anna is growing her hair out. It is not very long yet, it barely touches her shoulders, but she wants to put it up for tonight's going out, and she has asked her granddaughter to lend her a spare comb or a barrette. John is taking her to see a performance at the Odeon Theatre, the same play they saw on their first anniversary some forty years ago. On the bedroom dresser, there is a photograph of them in front of the same theater, taken when the theater was new and they were young. Anna wears a black dress patterned with small leaves. Her hair is up. John, straight as an arrow, seems very much aware of what a handsome couple they make. The photograph is black-and-white when no one looks closely at it. It is full of color and noise, however, if one stares at it for a few moments. John's eyes are bright blue, the little leaves on Anna's dress are green, and her hair shines, dark brown with some red brought out by daily rinsing with hibiscus brew. Ancient looking motorcars rattle the cobbles of the pavement, the roasted chestnuts merchant cries his wares, and Anna's laughter can be heard clearly over the din.

John is already dressed and is waiting in the living room, reading today's paper, which he had saved for that purpose. He is not allowed into the bedroom until Anna calls him; she has a surprise for him. She is going to wear the very same dress she wore back then. They both have kept most of the good clothes they have ever owned—the quality of the materials is just not the same anymore—so she has on the black dress patterned with pale green leaves. The dress had needed only a slight alternation around the waist, and the silk hugs Anna's figure quite nicely.

Anna turns to one side and studies her profile in the mirror. She doesn't like her elbows and tries to cover them with the sleeves, but they are too short for that. The combs and barrettes her granddaughter brought are spread out on the dresser. Among the cheap plastic ones, there are two that may work. One is made of silver wire. It has a large twirl in the middle and two smaller ones on both sides. The other is enamel-covered copper, dark green and glossy. It is shaped like a dragonfly. Anna reaches for it. It will go well with her dress and with her half-gray, half-brown hair.

"Growing out my hair has nothing to do with the incident," she assures her granddaughter all of a sudden. She is not reading the girl's thoughts—her granddaughter isn't thinking about that—Anna is not even addressing her. She is saying it aloud so she can believe in its truthfulness herself, even though she knows that her hair has everything to do with the incident, no matter how hard she has tried to persuade the neighbors that it is nothing but a caprice. The incident still burns brightly like a candle on a shelf in her mind where she keeps her troublesome memories.

Anna and John have an exemplary marriage that was tarnished only once, and by no fault of theirs. It hadn't been exactly personal, either, since all the men from the neighborhood were guilty of the same transgression. Half of the neighborhood still blames it on the Russian; the other half, on Mara the Deaf.

No one knows how the other women reacted to the common threat, but Anna stopped talking to John for three days, and only after he developed big, red blisters all over his body from anxiety and fret did she break her silence. "So, you've been thinking about Mara the Deaf."

He knew instantly what she meant. She was

accusing him that in her intimate presence he was thinking about another woman.

Mara the Deaf was a tall, willowy woman who smiled all the time, even when alone. Since she was deaf, she was left outside the daily gossip, and that afforded her an aura of sainthood that was impossible to achieve otherwise. Her innocence gave her a youthful look, and she was the only woman in her age group who still wore her hair long. She usually braided it tightly, but when seen loose, it was beautiful hair indeed, falling around her shoulders in honey-colored waves, the gray frothing on them as they went down. The rest of the women had terrible haircuts and chemical perms, coiling and uncoiling semiannually as they visited Lalka, the local hairdresser.

John didn't fail to grasp the gravity of the accusation. There was a long, tortured silence. Anna even felt a little sorry for him and wondered what was on his mind. Possibly, he wished he had skipped his visit to the Senior Citizens' Club that night. But he hadn't. He had been there, along with the rest of them, having a peaceful game of backgammon with his best friend, the Russian, when Mara's husband drew the winning raffle ticket. He won a bottle of twelve-year-old cab and a five-pound bag of last year's crop of almonds.

"Lucky bastard," the Russian said in a casual manner. "And this on top of having a deaf wife."

"What's so good about having a deaf wife?" someone asked.

"Well," the Russian said, taking a long draw from his cigarette, a Chesterfield, no filter, "He could talk dirty to her, and she would never know it."

The old gents laughed, as this was a good joke, but the thought of whispering dirty words in Mara's ear had already started making its way into their minds like whirls of honey-colored smoke, frosted just a little with gray, and soon they found themselves thinking of nothing else. For the next two weeks one could see John and the rest of them strolling around the neighborhood, buying the daily newspaper, or waiting for time to pass over a cup of coffee, with the dreamy expression of teenagers in love. If one met their eyes, one could see Mara's face there, smiling her innocent smile.

How could they possibly think they could get away with that?

John had paid his reparations, one small token after the other, throughout the whole winter. He fixed everything that needed fixing in the house, and more than once he drove to the neighboring town to buy the best persimmons there were, for Anna was very fond of persimmons. When spring came, he prepared her vegetable garden with utmost care. He attacked the soil with such vigor that the night crawlers ran from under his spade and sought shelter in the roots of the cassis bushes. He turned the soil over twice and fluffed it with a hoe until it started foaming like rich cream. It rained the next day, and the soil seemed to boil with impatience, effervescent with desire for the seeds and the small plants started indoors three months earlier and now wilting in the kitchen window. Anna took pity on the seedlings. She planted them in the late afternoon so they could sleep in their new beds before meeting the sun for the first time. The soil was so ready to receive them that all Anna had to do was to take the seedlings out of the plastic cups and place them in rows. With a distinct fizzing sound, the soil sucked them in, tightened around them, and settled still. Anna gathered the plastic cups and went in to start dinner, giving John, who had observed the scene from the back porch, only a small nod.

The memory of his expression back then—half hopeful, half forlorn—makes Anna smile. Her granddaughter wants to know why, but the evening sound of church bells comes through the open window, colliding with her words and changing their meaning, until it seems to Anna that the girl is answering a question, not asking one.

John walks into the room. "The taxi is waiting," he says. He wears a double-breasted brown suit, a cream shirt and a silk tie, clipped with a silver, hand-made clasp.

Anna looks at him, hands the green comb to her granddaughter and takes the silver one instead. She pulls her hair back, twisting it in a knot, and pins it with the comb. With a little shake of her head, she makes sure the knot is stable, then she pulls John next to her and makes him look in the mirror. In the twilight, they look almost like they do in the old photograph. He, tall and straight as an arrow. She, slight and shapely. The blue has faded from John's eyes, and Anna's skin has lost its translucent olive color, but in a way that doesn't make them look old, just interminable.

They study their reflection for a long time, having forgotten the waiting taxi and their granddaughter's presence in the room. The girl gets up to leave. On her way out, she reaches to turn the lights on, but Anna stops her. "Please, don't," she says. "We are going any moment now."

A horn sounds outside.

PARASKEVA'S GHOST

There she was again, not in the middle of my room, her usual spot, but slightly to the side, as if to cause as much damage to the carpet as possible with the inexhaustible water dripping from her clothes and hair. For a moment, I wondered which was less disturbing to look at—her swollen fingers bent in unnatural angles with shards of bone protruding through the skin, or her bruised legs, a hose twisted around one ankle, the soaked rim of her dress leaking streaks of indigo-blue color down her pasty flesh. For sure, it was not her head, and closing my eyes wasn't an option. When I did that last night, she came to stand above me, and the blood squirting from the wound on her forehead mixed with the mud in her hair and came down on my face in long, sticky drops. I had jumped out of my bed and begged her to move away so she wouldn't ruin my pillow and sheets, but she stood there for the rest of her visit.

"How may I help you?" I asked, not expecting an answer—she hadn't spoken once in the previous five nights—but out of inbred propriety. I so wished my grandma was home. Maybe she would know who this woman was and why her ghost had come to bother me. But Grandma was enjoying her mineral baths, and I had to deal with all this alone, every night playing guessing games, every morning dabbing the muddy carpet with towels, and mopping the water from the hardwood floors in the entry and the living room. I had to agree that it was polite for a ghost to enter through the front door, but on the other hand, I was afraid that the moisture would lift the parquet pieces and ruin the floors. Which reminded me to ask the ghost a favor.

"Excuse me, ma'am. Would you mind draping yourself with the blanket over there?"

She stared at me with her usual stare, blank and solemn at the same time, not giving any indication she had heard me. I knew better than to get angry. However, the situation was starting to wear me out.

I took a deep breath and spoke slowly, carefully enunciating each word, trying not to shout. "Who-are-you? What-do-you-want-from-me?"

The woman lifted a hand to her face and moaned. I couldn't understand what she meant; each of her broken fingers pointed in a different direction.

"What?" This time I shouted. "Open your mouth and speak up, damn it!"

She opened her mouth. A dense flow of hemorrhaged blood carrying chunks of flesh and broken teeth spilled down her chin.

That served me right.

"Sorry...I am very sorry. Please, close your mouth. Ma'am, please. Maybe you could nod?"

The woman closed her mouth and nodded.

"Thank you," I said, and went on asking my questions. Was I supposed to know her, was she a relation of mine, did she want dry clothes or anything to eat (I was smart enough to not offer her water), and did she have a message for somebody, to all of which she slowly shook her head from side to side. I wished she would wipe the blood from her chin, but she didn't.

Finally, the first rooster crowed, and before the rest of them had a chance to join in, the ghost was gone. I thought for a moment about the soaked carpet and the wet floors, but couldn't make myself get up and start cleaning. Tomorrow, I would put plastic sheets all the way from the front door to my room, three feet wide at least.

When I woke up, around ten, the sun had just reached the damp spot on the carpet, and greenish vapors filled the room. The air was rich with smells of acidic soil, stale water, blooming cattails and manna grass. The tang of decomposing matter mixed with the sweet fragrance of calamus leaves, reminding me of the marshes along the river.

I cleaned the mess, took a shower, and after opening all windows and interior doors, and turning on the fan in the living room, I left the house.

Mrs. Quince, the next-door neighbor, had already installed her scrawny self at her watching post—on the front porch of her house, partially hidden behind the boxes with begonias. She didn't notice me. She seemed to be nodding off.

Farther along the street, Mr. K. Bayo and Mr. J. Bayo, the twins, were fighting dandelions on their front lawn. They appeared more inept than usual, and seeing me, used the opportunity to abandon the weeds. They crossed the lawn with their identical, jerky gaits and came to a tentative halt in the shade of the magnolia tree.

"Mrs. Quince is asleep on her porch, and you don't look your cheerful selves," I said. "Did something happen?"

"Oh, nothing much," Mr. K. Bayo, the older twin, said, wiping his bald dome with a huge, checkered handkerchief. "Only the masons made an ungodly amount of noise last night, and no one in the neighborhood got enough sleep. I mean us, the oldsters. You probably slept through all the '…more sand…more bricks…pass the mortar hoe,' but at some point I was about to be rude and tell them to shut up."

"Talking about ghosts, I had a little problem myself. Do you happen to know about a woman who drowned in the area?"

"Many people, both men and women, drowned in the time of the flood, nineteen-fifty-seven," Mr. K. Bayo said. Being the older of the two, he did all the talking. "Can you tell by her clothes if she lived then?"

"No. Maybe. Her clothes are plastered about her body, and so wet, I couldn't even tell what color they had been. And I've never heard of any of the flood victims haunting the town. It seems kind of late to start doing so after more than fifty years, don't you think?"

"You should've asked her," Mr. J. Bayo said all of a sudden. His voice sounded stronger and clearer than the voice of his brother as if he had preserved it by not using it.

It took me awhile to overcome my surprise. "I did ask her. She wouldn't tell me anything. Most of all, I want to know what made her choose our house. I am sure there has been a mistake."

"Hardly a mistake," Mr. J. Bayo said. "The only two houses in town not haunted presently are yours and Mrs. Quince's. Do you think anyone, living or otherwise, would want to move in with Mrs. Quince?"

"That's a good point, but…Can't you take her?

You have only your mum's ghost to haunt you, don't you?"

"It won't work," Mr. J. Bayo said, almost wistfully. "Mum doesn't get along with girls."

Mr. K. Bayo coughed. It sounded as if he was trying to clear his throat of rusty nails. "Off with you, Reni. Didn't you say you are on your way to the library?" he said, and turned to his brother, "Come on, Jeleb. The heat is insufferable. I can barely stand on my feet."

They went into the house, and I went to the library where I asked Miss Mona for the "Statistics, Particulars, and Curiosities of Kirpich" by the locally renowned historian St. Kvasin.

"Kirpich is a small picturesque town in the foothills of the Balkan Mountains," I read. "It has 15,678 inhabitants according to the last count (1968). The citizens think they are just as refined and sophisticated as the people living in cities with populations of up to 100,000. Which is definitely true." It went like that for about twenty pages before I reached the part that interested me. "The town has one of the largest per capita ghost manifestations. No less than two thousand five hundred ghosts haunt residences and public areas. For a detailed description and haunting habits, see Appendix B."

I leafed to Appendix B and spent an hour-and-a-half going through the list. The masons were classified under "Fratricides, Double, Trivial." The two brothers had decided to build a house together, on the lot next to Mrs. Quince's house—the lot stood empty since— but had quarreled before the walls were all the way up and killed each other with their masonry tools. Now their ghosts could be heard on clear nights going about finishing the house, shouting orders and requests at each other and robbing a whole neighborhood of peaceful sleep.

Fatima, the other communal ghost, was listed under "Suicides, Love, Unshared."

The coachman that cruised the streets from one end of the town to the other, beating his horses mercilessly, was under "Revenges, Love, Lost." I disliked his ghost, but thankfully, it was easy to avoid a chance encounter—wheels screeched, horseshoes met the asphalt casting sparks, dogs howled in its wake.

I found twenty-six cases of death by drowning, accidental and intentional, none of which referred to the ghost in my room.

The Kirpich Times Call was housed just two blocks from the library. I walked there and placed an ad to appear for the next three days in Lost & Found: "A ghost of a drowned woman, circa nineteen-fifty-seven. Any information appreciated. Reward."

Imagine who called the next day? My grandmother.

"Why didn't you tell me about the ghost?" she asked.

"How did you hear about it?"

"Well, what do you think? We have computers in the lobby—actually, one computer, the other one is always broken—and I read the paper online every morning."

"Grandma, I didn't want to spoil your vacation, but since you know already…." I told her all about the ghost, the wet clothes, the puffy flesh, the twigs in her hair. I skipped the part with the muddy water dripping onto the floors.

"Twigs in her hair? What was her hair like?" Grandma asked.

"Hmm, loose, maybe dark."

"What do you mean by maybe?"

"I don't know. She has mud all over—"

"Clothes?"

"Knee-length, three-quarter sleeves."

"It doesn't ring a bell," Grandma said, and then her voice became muffled as if she had covered the phone to talk to somebody there. When I thought we had been disconnected, she spoke with a high-pitched, girlish voice I almost didn't recognized, "Sorry, dear, my bingo is starting in a minute. Just keep the ghost happy until I come home. Talk to you soon."

She called again in the evening, just as I was starting to fret. "Check with the Vlaevs," she said. "River Street Number 80, second house east of the dike. The old Vlaev lost his wife in the flood. No one blamed him—he couldn't swim, and even though the water was only neck-deep, the current was really strong down there. The rumors were that he had climbed up a pear tree, watching from there as the water carried away his wife, screaming and begging for help. He never admitted being haunted, but still, it's worth a try."

"Thanks, Grandma."

"Ciao, dear. See you on Wednesday."

"I thought you were coming back tomorrow!"

"Change of plans. Need to practice my samba a bit more," she said, and giggled.

I looked at the frozen dinner still rotating in the microwave, and deciding a delay couldn't make it any more tasteless, I hurried through town, down to River Street Number 80.

At least I knew one of the Vlaevs—Ivaylo. He was a senior in my school, a year ahead of me. He had once asked me out, and when I refused, he stopped speaking to me. I hoped he had forgotten about it.

When I rang the bell, it was Ivaylo who opened the door. He pretended he didn't know who I was and said, "We do not appreciate soliciting at dinner time."

"I haven't come to sell you things. I need to talk to your parents."

"What about?"

"None of your business," I said, and rang the bell again. Finally, Ivaylo's mother came to the door.

"Do you have a ghost missing from the household?" I inquired politely.

"What are you talking about?"

"A drowned lady, short, stocky, lots of mud. My grandmother seems to think she was your mother-in-law."

The woman started choking, recovered quickly, and waved her arms in fake outrage. "Ha! What nonsense. Go away, girl, and don't bother us again."

The door closed. I stood there, my hand halfway up to knock, unsure what to do. I've never heard of anyone disowning a family ghost. In a town with so many of them, there were unspoken rules and regulations of conduct. No one dared to insult a ghost, no matter if in residence or a communal one. No one turned their back and slept through the visitations without at least offering an explanation. I knew some people made excuses with work the next day or tests in school, but it had to be a really good reason or they paid the price later.

What did the Vlaevs think they were? An exception?

I knocked on the door, rang the bell a few times, and when no one answered, I shouted through the mail slot, "You better come and collect her tonight, or…or…" I didn't know what I would do if they didn't show up. Call the police? Expose them at the town's meeting? Write to the editor?

I went back home, ate the adhesive blob that my dinner had turned into, and used all the plastic bags left in the box to cover the floors. I had barely finished when the ghost stepped in, dragging her feet and dragging along my plastic bags, which were too thin and too flimsy, and stuck to the mud on her soles.

"Excuse me…excuse me," I kept repeating while trying to hold the edges of the bags down pressing them with my big toe. I pointed to the chair covered with towels that I had prepared earlier and called the Vlaevs. I didn't care at all that it was after midnight.

"Who is it?" Ivaylo asked. His voice was slurred. In the background, I could hear music and chatter.

"Having a party, yeah?" I said. "A celebration, I guess?"

There was a short silence, then, "It's Saturday, Reni. What do you expect me to do?"

"I expect you to come over and fetch your grandmother's ghost. Haven't you any shame?"

"Are you crazy? Or stupid? Why would I want to do such a thing?" The noise from the party died. Ivaylo was drunk, but not drunk enough to let his friends hear what he was about to tell me. "Do you know how much trouble she's been? Because of her, we had to tile all the floors. Every night, we had to roll up the carpets and lift them onto the tables or prop them along the walls. Do you think that was fun?"

"But she is yours. It's not my fault that your grandfather let her drown."

"I don't care. My dad doesn't care, and my mom doesn't care the smallest bit. You are stuck, Reni."

"What about your grandfather? Doesn't he care?"

"The old fool has no say in the matter. By the way, he won't be around much longer—he is going to a nursing home. No more spending his whole pension on wine to drink at night with the damned ghost."

Ivaylo slammed the phone hard but must have missed the slot, because I could hear him swearing under his breath, then opening a door and shouting, "Is there any beer left?"

I turned around. The ghost sat at the edge of her chair, shivering, and looking more miserable if that were possible.

"Sorry," I said. "No one is available at the moment. Please make yourself comfortable. I'll be right back."

I hadn't undressed yet, so I only needed my sandals. One of them was close to the ghost's right foot, which she moved an inch or two to allow me to take my sandal without the discomfort of reaching into her aura. "Appreciated," I muttered and left the house, this time in no particular hurry.

In the middle of the street, Fatima, the ghost of the Turkish woman who had thrown herself into the neighborhood well, sat on the asphalt with her legs crossed under her. Since they had filled the well in 1986 when the city paved the street, Fatima had nowhere to sit but on the ground. She hadn't been an unhappy ghost before, I was told, sitting on the ledge of the well, tinkling the bangles on her wrists, and greeting the late night passersby with a soft "Assalamu Alaikum." These days she kept her eyes down, her hands limp in her lap, and her bangles silent. Usually she sat very still, but tonight she was rocking her upper body as if in trance, back and forth, back and forth.

"Good evening, Fatima," I said. She didn't answer, just kept rocking. I took a good look at her. Even taking into account the shimmer and the luminescent transparency of her body and clothes, I could see that she didn't have a drop of water on her. She had jumped to her death into the well, probably hitting the stone walls on her way down, and definitely drowning in the water, but her clothes were dry, her face wasn't marked with bruises, and her hairpiece neatly covered her hair.

Deep in thought, I didn't hear the warning thunder of hooves and barely had time to flatten myself against a fence when the coachman came down the street. The coach leaped behind the galloping horses, the coachman cracking his long whip over their haunches and howling in full voice, "Giddyap! Giddyap!" as if they could possibly run any faster. The coachman's features were distorted with rage but clear of blemishes, even though he had found his end tumbling down a 200 foot deep ravine. I tried not to look at the horses, wretched beasts, frothing and showing their teeth, the whites of their bulging, horrified eyes iridescent in the light of the half moon.

When we were in elementary school, my best friend and I collected signatures and tried to interest PETA in the inhumane treatment of the ghost horses, but no one returned our calls.

After that encounter, I proceeded more carefully, and managed to cross the town without meeting the coachman again. Just as I was about to turn into River Street, I heard him coming from the opposite end. I made a quick escape, cutting through somebody's backyard and climbing the dike. He wouldn't follow me here. I knew that for sure—he cruised only the streets and roads that had existed at the time of his death. The dike along the river was built in 1958, after the big flood.

As I walked along the dike, the houses down on my left, the river on my right, I thought about the flood. I remembered it with the false memory of an impressionable child, in the colors of the yellowed newspapers I've seen in the basement. If I closed my eyes, I could see the old tsar wading through the muddy water and the floating corpses.

I must have really closed my eyes, because when I opened them, I was standing on nothing, five feet up in the air. The dike had disappeared. The river was roaring under my feet.

Vertigo and disorientation overwhelmed me. I swayed in place, afraid that if I made just one step away from my invisible platform, I'd fall in the water. "What is going on?" I cried. "This is not supposed to be happening!"

Maybe I would have kept yapping like a lost puppy if the cool, prickly presence of a ghost hadn't brought me back to my senses. It was the ghost of the drowned woman. She lifted her hand and pointed at the distance. A ten-foot wall of murky water was rushing down the riverbed. The ghost made sure I saw it and pointed down, at the houses. If I were not mistaken, one of her broken fingers was aligned with the Vlaevs' house.

Eerie light replaced the illumination of the occasional streetlight. Actually, the streetlights, along with the posts they were attached to, had disappeared. Some of the houses remained the same, others were gone, and a few that I didn't remember sprouted up in the vacated spaces. There were no street trees, no sidewalks, and even the concrete pavement was replaced with cobbles. At last, I understood. The ghost wanted me to see what had happened to her back in 1957.

The wall of water hit the first houses, parted around them and flew into the streets and the yards, uprooting small trees, hauling up cars, household items, a horse cart along with the struggling horse, people—men, women, small children. Birds abandoned their nests, filling the sky with black wings. Cats climbed on the roofs. The dogs in the dog runs didn't stand a chance.

"I can't… I can't watch anymore…I can't stand it." I turned my head, preferring to look the ghost in the face but not the horror unfolding around me, but the ghost's hand kept pointing with its broken fingers, and I had no power to refuse.

The water was no deeper than four or five feet now, but it seemed to flow even faster. A man's voice hollering, "Paraskeva! Paraskeva!" drew my attention to the Vlaevs' yard. First, I saw the man only. He was up a pear tree, leaning at a dangerous angle over the water. He straightened for a moment, only to take off his belt and wrap it around a branch, then he took the other end and leaned even farther. Now, he was two feet closer to the water but still not close enough to reach the young woman holding to the trunk of the tree. Waves rolled over her head one after another. Every time her head bobbed up, she gasped desperately for air, water streaming from her nostrils and mouth, waiting for the next wave to come and hit her. Still, it seemed she was going to make it. She hugged the tree with the fervor of a lover, and a branch the man had bent down was within her reach.

She waited for the right moment, concentrating on the task, not noticing the two barrels that just popped out of the basement. The water carried them across the yard so swiftly that when she saw them it was too late. One of them hit the tree trunk, smashing her hands into a bloody mass. The other one caught her on the side of the head.

"Paraskeva..."

It all became still. The dike rose from under my feet, the streetlights flickered as if just lit, the houses slept, and the river was only a silvery ribbon winding through the purple shadows of the jacaranda trees.

I sighed. So that was that. But what was it? What did it mean? I turned to look at Paraskeva's ghost, but her expression was unreadable. She had shown me what she wanted me to see, and now it was up to me to draw the conclusions. Sorry as I felt for her, it had been Ivaylo's grandfather who didn't manage to save his wife. I wasn't going to get stranded with her ghost.

Making sure the coachman was not in sight, I climbed down the dike, crossed the back alley, and jumped the low fence around the Vlaevs' backyard. It was darker here than up on the dike. I stumbled through a vegetable garden, my feet stirring the fragrance of mint and crushed tomato leaves. The two-story house loomed above me with its black windows. Somebody coughed, a dry hacking cough that came from a smaller building to the left, a detached garage. Dim light squeezed out from under the door. I turned the knob, expecting to find Ivaylo's father polishing his golf clubs or whatever the guy did after midnight in his garage. Instead, I found a very old man lying on a narrow bed, covered to the chin with a dirty comforter. A table and a single chair completed the furnishings. The bastards! They had put the old man to live in the garage!

"Paraskeva," the old man spoke. He wasn't looking at me, but to the side. I turned and saw Paraskeva's ghost sitting on a big, old fashioned suitcase next to the door. "Sorry, sweetheart, they won't let you visit me in the nursing home. It's against their policy—I asked the nurse that came to fill out the papers. No spirits of any kind, she said. Ah, what are we going to do?"

Paraskeva's ghost pointed at me. The old man saw me for the first time and slow understanding started to creep up his face. Not allowing him even a moment of hope, I cried, "No! I am sorry. We don't have the accommodations."

The old man started sobbing quietly, tears running down his hollow cheeks, disappearing into the white bristles of his week-old beard.

Unable to take my eyes away from him, I stepped back, tripping on a loose piece of concrete and almost losing my balance. The concrete chip fit nicely in the palm of my hand. I swung it with all my strength and sent it flying at one of the second-story windows. The crash splintered the quiet, and the Vlaevs' shouts and cusses came through shredded and unrecognizable.

I ran the whole way home. Last I saw Paraskeva's ghost, she was sitting on her husband's suitcase, but fast as I ran, she still beat me to my room. I dropped another towel around her feet, and barely having the strength to remove my sandals, I fell into my bed.

The next three days I lived my life in very small increments. I took small steps everywhere I went, sipped small sips of water when thirsty, cut my bread into miniature bites, and answered questions with yes or no.

At last, Wednesday came and at six-twenty-five, a very ancient taxicab delivered my grandmother and her numerous bags in front of our house. I had been waiting there for the bigger part of the afternoon. Grandma patted me on the cheek and said, "There, there, it couldn't be all that bad," but when we got inside, she seemed to think otherwise. "Oh my," she said, and after a short moment of indecisiveness, she rolled her sleeves up, noting, "Good thinking about the plastic bags."

It took Grandma two hours to clean the house, air the rooms, and make dinner. Around nine-thirty, she fed me my first home-cooked meal in the past eighteen days, and told me to get lost. Not in these words, but the meaning was clear. She needed to be alone with the ghost, and I had to go and entertain myself elsewhere.

I went to the rock club and drank diet sodas until closing time. It was two in the morning when I finally headed home. The closer I got, the faster my heart beat, about to explode when I took the last turn. Fatima was already there, seated in the middle of the street. "Assalamu Alaikum," she said, and when I answered, she gave me a little wave. The bangles on her wrist jingled. It seemed like a good sign. I felt a little better.

Grandma had left the porch light on. Otherwise, the house was dark. I opened the front door, starting to hope for the best. Releasing a long breath, I reached for the light switch. "He, he, he," I heard my grandmother's laughter from the direction of the kitchen. My hand froze in the air. Holding my breath again, I tiptoed through the living room and looked into the kitchen.

At the table, Grandma and Paraskeva's ghost chatted amiably. More precisely, Grandma chatted and the ghost nodded, her crooked fingers wrapped around the stem of one of my grandmother's second-best sherry glasses. Grandma had a glass, too. Between the two of them, the liquid in the decanter shone like a lava lamp.

My grandma must have sensed my presence, because she said over her shoulder, "Don't worry, dear. We have an arrangement with Paraskeva—she will be entering through the kitchen door and will try to keep to the lawn chair."

Paraskeva's ghost was, indeed, seated in one of our plastic lawn chairs.

"But, Grandma," I whined. "She looks so...er...untidy. And she drips water."

"Her appearance will improve as soon as her husband passes away—doesn't it happen to all of us?" Grandma said. "And a little water won't hurt the linoleum. Besides, after twenty years of insomnia, there are not many books left that I care to read. Go to bed, dear, and don't give it a second thought."

Grandma turned to Paraskeva's ghost and continued the conversation, I mean the monologue, I had interrupted. "And then I told him, 'You are such a flatterer! I haven't danced for years.' And guess what he said?"

THE HOUSE WITH TWELVE ROOMS

One chilly morning in January, Mrs. Rilska sent for her nephew. The nephew was eighty-two at the time, sixteen years her junior. Being that much younger than his aunt, he didn't think of making excuses with the weather or with his leg giving him trouble, but started out as soon as he had finished his linden tea with bread and butter. He wiped the crumbs from his mustache, put on his lamb-fur cap, shook his pocket for coins and climbed the streets to the upper end of the village.

The nephew made just one stop, at the bakery, from where he emerged with two loaves of bread, one under each arm. The clock on the church tower struck ten by the time he reached the spacious house with as many as twelve rooms, where in the beginning of the century three generations had shared one roof, and where now his aunt occupied only the kitchen.

Six-foot stone walls enclosed the house, and the only way inside was through the small door carved in one of the panels of the great double gate. The gate that was wide enough to allow in three horsemen riding abreast and that needed two strong men to open it had been shut since nineteen forty-six. Today, his aunt had cleared the snow away in front of the whole gate as if she planned on opening it at last.

As the nephew slowed down, contemplating the curious snow removal, the small door opened, and Marco stepped out. He had his carpenter's box with him. What he had come for was not to fix something in the house as the nephew assumed, but to measure Mrs. Rilska for a casket, which she wanted by tomorrow morning. She had told Marco she was to die today. In Marco's opinion, she didn't seem on her way, but he was going to make the casket nonetheless. She was ninety-eight years old, and she would need it sooner rather than later.

The nephew bade Marco goodbye and went inside. He stomped his feet at the back door and entered the kitchen. Mrs. Rilska was in her bed, propped high on pillows and covered with a heap of blankets and shawls. She was knitting a sock.

"What took you so long?" she asked with

displeasure.

"Brought you some fresh bread," the nephew said, and dropped one of the loaves on the table. He kept the other loaf as he pulled a chair close to the stove. On the other side of the stove, a cat leaned so close to it that his whiskers could catch fire any moment. The cat was skin and bones, and looked much closer to death than Mrs. Rilska, who had good color on her face from the warmth in the room. The needles flew in her hands with their customary speed despite the arthritis Mrs. Rilska claimed to suffer.

"I need no bread. I will be dead by tonight, and I don't have a craving for food."

"Are you sure? I mean about the dying?" The nephew broke a big chunk from the loaf in his hands and chewed on it with his front teeth.

"Quite sure. Now don't waste my time. Listen to what I have to tell you." Mrs. Rilska let go of her knitting and pulled a picture from under her pillow. The picture was faded black and white, with frayed edges and a yellowish smear over most of it.

The nephew studied the two young girls in the photograph. They were clad in traditional folk costumes. These days, such costumes lay forgotten in old trunks here and there, worn only for the amusement of the tourists. The photograph must have been taken some eighty years ago.

"Which one is you?" The nephew asked, not

because he could recognize his aunt's wasted features in either of these smiling, fresh faces, but because it seemed logical that she would be in it. He had spent his youth away from the village and when he returned, his aunt was already an old woman.

Mrs. Rilska stood up with vigor one would not expect from the dying and chased away the cat, who had gotten on the table to sniff the bread. Then, she lay down again, arranged her blankets and shawls, and took the picture back from her nephew.

"This one is me," she said, pointing at the prettier girl, then pressed a brown, thickened nail over the other girl's face. "This one is Lilla, may she burn in hell, and may all of hers keep her company."

"Eh, Aunt, if you are dying, isn't it better to watch—"

"Shut up. I'll be with her before tonight, and I'll tell her the same thing." Mrs. Rilska reached under her blankets and rummaged through them for a while. She brought out a long string of gold coins. The coins had small holes through which the string was entwined. A very common way to keep one's gold, back in the day.

Mrs. Rilska shook the coins in her nephew's face.

"This is my pass to hell. I accepted the gold for my silence, and I didn't keep it. Now it's time for payback."

"Aunt, if you want to make a confession, we should call—"

"I don't seek absolution, and hell doesn't scare me," Mrs. Rilska said, her expression turning stubborn.

"Then what scares you? I never thought you feared anything."

Mrs. Rilska lowered her voice to a whisper. "The curse scares me. The zmay's curse. He cursed me so that neither heaven would not accept my soul, nor earth accept my body. I thought he was going to burn me alive and be done with it, but he cursed me. May his heart never know peace!"

"Aunt, not with the zmay again! There is no such thing. Only in myths and songs."

"That shows what you know. I've met one, may he rot alive!"

"You better stop cursing." The nephew looked around with discomfort. Not that he believed in zmay, but still.

"Don't tell me what to do. I'll curse him with my final breath. You just pay attention now." Mrs. Rilska settled in her shawls and beckoned the nephew to come closer. When he dragged his chair an inch or two in her direction, she pointed with her needle at Lilla's face on the picture. "When I was seventeen and she was nineteen, as you know, we married two brothers. We lived in this same house with our parents-in-law. At first, I was confident in my advantages over her. I was prettier, I was younger, I could spin wool like no one else, and my first child was a boy, while she gave her husband a girl, small and dark-haired like herself.

My golden hair, my fair skin, and all my skills didn't do me any good, however. Lilla was a trickster. She would walk the eighteen kilometers to town to bring our mother-in-law menthol drops for her stomach. She would gather herbs to fill everybody's pillows so we could have sweet dreams. When our father-in-law came home, she would be the first one to meet him at the gates. She would hold his horse for him to dismount. She would bring him a basin with water and a towel to wash away the dust from the road. She would sing for him when he lost a sheep in the mountains or a game of cards in the tavern. People are stupid to fall for things like that, but they do."

Mrs. Rilska jerked at her yarn to untangle the knots that had formed there and continued, "I didn't hold it against her. When she started coming home late, disheveled and her eyes shining, it was I who tried to warn her. 'Don't mess with other men,' I told her. 'Nothing good will come out of that.' She told me she was sorry, but there was nothing she could do. A zmay loved her, she said, not a mere man. Of course, I didn't believe her. I thought, just like you do, that this happened only in songs and fairy tales, and there wasn't such a creature as a zmay. Still, I wanted to know whom she was seeing.

One day when it was her turn to take the goats to the upland pastures, I followed her. She stopped at the spring-capture and washed her face and her feet. A silk scarf replaced the cotton one on her head, and she picked wildflowers to put in her hair and in the ties of the scarf. She liked to have her hair braided into eight braids so they were thinner and lighter and twisted around her waist when she walked. She had done it in this fashion that day. I hurried after her, hiding behind trees, slipping and getting thorns in my clothes, and watching that damned hair of hers whirl around her like a cluster of snakes. I almost lost her, once or twice, she was so eager to get there.

When I reached the wood's edge, I saw her standing in the middle of the pasture, the goats running all over—a miracle she hadn't lost any—and she looking up as if she really expected her lover to come from above. I thought that she had lost her mind and felt relieved. But then, oh, I would never forget the first time I saw him. He appeared as if from nowhere, and the beating of his wings made the treetops bend to the ground. His wings were see-through and varicolored like a rainbow seen in moonlight. I saw his heart beat with fire, and he was more beautiful and more fearsome than Archangel Michael. He landed next to Lilla, and they embraced as no man and woman had embraced before. While covering her face with kisses, he changed. The wings disappeared, and his flesh became solid and human-like. His bare arms were so strong and so handsome, and I so wished such arms around me that I cried.

Through my tears, I saw him letting go of Lilla and coming my way. I closed my eyes and wished that he would kiss me before he killed me. He did neither. He pulled me out from behind the tree and waited for me to open my eyes. "Whatever you want, you shall have it. Now go." Just like that.

"You asked for gold?"

"No, I didn't. I didn't ask for anything. I offered to come with Lilla every time and keep watch. And I did come many times. I wouldn't spy on them, I'd be on the rock where the trail splits, watching out for people. The zmay didn't need my services. He could smell the people. He could hide in a cloud and become invisible. He could breathe fire and make a thunderstorm come from a clear sky. He could do anything he wanted. The only thing he was powerless to do was to persuade Lilla to leave her child behind and go with him.

He thought I might help him. Once he asked me if I would. I couldn't help myself. I fell at his feet and begged him to take me instead. He laughed at me and petted me as if I were some puppy. I went to my rock that day, and when he was leaving, the first coin dropped into my lap. What I did for love, now I was doing for pay."

"Well, at least you made some profit out of this," the nephew said.

"You have always been a fool," Mrs. Rilska said. "You know what happened next, people still talk. Four people died, the flood and the fire destroyed half of the village, the wheat in the cellars got wet, and until spring we ate bread that smelled like mildew."

"How did it come to this? Did you tell her husband?"

"Worse. I told her father. He put a hole through her chest with his Mannlicher, that big."

"So, the flood was the zmay's revenge?"

"No, it wasn't. If it were his revenge, we all would have been dead, and there wouldn't be a stone left from the village. It was his grief that caused the devastation."

The nephew waited, but this seemed to be the end of the story.

"What do you want me to do, Aunt?"

"About the funeral there is not much for you to do. I have prepared. You'll need to call Father Profirii to do the rites, I don't want the other one—what's his name—he sings off key. Call him as soon as you get home so he has time to sober up by tomorrow. For Veneta's funeral last month, he came sloshed. On your way back, stop by Marco's and remind him about the casket. It should be here first thing in the morning. The women know how to braid my hair and tie my scarf, but make sure they've done a good job. The clothes are over there."

A change of clothes lay on the trunk. White wool socks with blue edging, linen undershirt with embroidery on the front, black dress never worn before, thin leather belt with belt buckles filigreed with silver, and a fine pair of pig-skin slippers.

Mrs. Rilska spoke one more time. "There is nothing you can do for my soul. But you can make sure I am properly buried—and stay that way." Then, she stretched her right hand for the nephew to kiss. He jumped out of his chair and bent over the brown-spotted, bony hand, small and fragile like a bird's. Her skin scrunched like old parchment under his lips.

Early next morning, while the nephew was having his tea, sugary and rich in butter, the church bells rang. The nephew counted the rings. One, two. Two rings announced that a woman had died. The nephew hurried with his breakfast; there was work to do.

By noon the doctor had come and pronounced Mrs. Rilska dead, the gravedigger had dug the grave, Father Profirii had sung the rites in the house and then at the graveside, and by four o'clock, Mrs. Rilska had been buried. The procession that included everyone from the village with the exception of Marco who fainted at funerals left the cemetery in haste just short of disrespectful, chased by a sudden windstorm. It brought warm air in the midst of January that melted the snow before midnight, and by the next day rain was pouring as if the bottom had fallen out of the sky. It rained like that the whole day. Muddy water flowed in the streets and got in the cellars. The houses in the lower end of the village flooded. The roofs started leaking, and all household pots and pans had to be placed under the leaks.

That night, the nephew dreamt of Mrs. Rilska. She was dripping wet. Fish swam around her through the soggy air and nibbled on her face. The nephew didn't like his dream, and first thing in the morning, he put on his rubber boots and his raincoat, and walked through the mud. It took him an hour to get to the cemetery, and he was there just in time to see a three-foot wall of water coming down the slope and splashing over the graves. As the nephew watched, a whirlpool formed over Mrs. Rilska's grave, a fountain of loosened dirt shot high, and Mrs. Rilska's casket popped out and was carried away with the torrent.

Farther down, the stream that in summer could barely house the frogs now roared, filled to the brim. Debris rolled along with the water and got caught in the arches of the bridge. If a good chance had it, the casket would get caught there, too. The nephew cleaned some of the mud from his boots and rushed after the casket. His boots got heavy again after a few steps, and his knee was threatening to give out, but the nephew ran as fast as an eighty-two-year-old man could run. He swore abundantly when he saw the casket moving away from the bridge, bobbing up and down, bumping into floating branches, and disappearing from view at the curve of the river. He ran another step or two, slipped, gave a loud cry, and grabbed for the brambles to slow down his fall.

As he slid toward the rushing water, the world around him blurred. The tree trunks turned into mighty legs, the bark into feathery scales, and the air shimmered like a rainbow seen in moonlight. Through the wall of rain, a pair of luminous eyes stared down at him. The nephew clawed at the dirt with the last of his strength, and finally came to a stop. He lay at the water's edge for a long time, his heart skipping, and his breath whistling. Then, he limped home, changed into dry clothes, and had four shots of homemade grappa.

In the next two weeks, Mrs. Rilska's casket was seen a number of times along the rivers that merge together on their way to the great Danube. People from the nearby towns gathered to see it passing. Kids went running and cheering along the shores. Men took their hats off and crossed themselves. Women threw stones after the casket and spat in the water. Fishing boats threw nets trying to catch it, but couldn't, and the casket went on its way to the Black Sea and farther, wherever the zmay's curse would take it.

The nephew brought scraps to Mrs. Rilska's cat every other day and tried to keep the house well aired and ready—after all, Mrs. Rilska's soul had nowhere else to go. Despite his efforts, the cat turned feral and hissed at him, and the house acquired a musty odor as if fungus was growing inside the walls. Opening the windows didn't help. Instead of light getting in, gloominess leaked out and speckled the fresh snow with gray that looked a lot like ashes. The nephew kicked at the snow, scratching thoughtfully the back of his neck, and wondering at the malignancy of womenfolk's feuds that can cause a perfectly good house to go to waste.

One day, he stepped into the cellar and came back with a hatful of nails. When all the windows and the front door were nailed shut, he left through the kitchen door and fished out the key. The key, having rusted under the hiding stone for years, broke inside the keyhole. The nephew tossed the leftover piece, shook the doorknob to make sure it was properly locked, and started across the yard.

Behind him, the house with the twelve rooms whined. It was a thin, high-pitched sound of the kind that the nephew had long ago lost the ability to hear. Slowly at first, with small jerky motions, then more resolutely, the house started folding into itself, losing shape but gaining substance and sinking into the ground. At the great double gate, the nephew turned to look at it one last time, only to see the top of the chimney vanishing so fast that the crows nesting in there barely had time to escape.